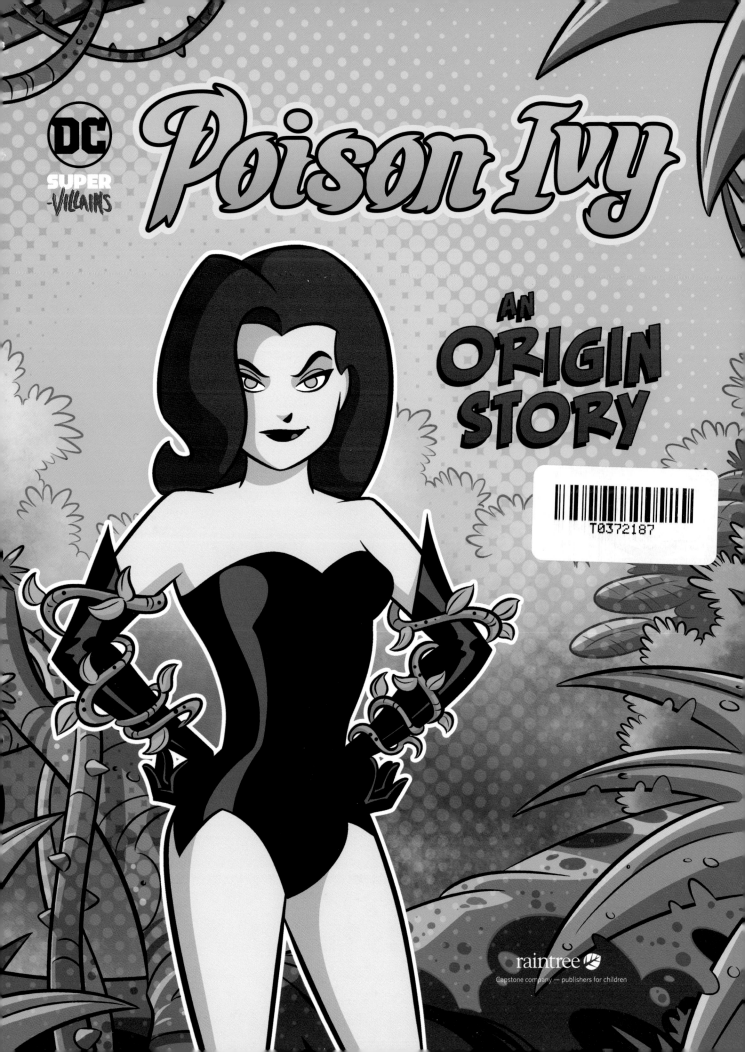

Raintree is an imprint of Capstone Global Library Limited, a company incorporated in England and Wales having its registered office at 264 Banbury Road, Oxford, OX2 7DY – Registered company number: 6695582

www.raintree.co.uk
myorders@raintree.co.uk

Designed by Hilary Wacholz
Originated by Capstone Global Library Ltd

978 1 3982 4444 3 (hardback)
978 1 3982 4443 6 (paperback)

British Library Cataloguing in Publication Data
A full catalogue record for this book is available from the British Library.

Printed and bound in India

Poison Ivy

AN ORIGIN STORY

WRITTEN BY
LAURIE S. SUTTON

ILLUSTRATED BY
DARIO BRIZUELA

BATMAN CREATED BY
BOB KANE WITH BILL FINGER

"Roses are red, violets are blue," little Pamela Isley sings. "I love my plants, and they love me too."

The girl sits in her parents' garden. Flowers rise up all around her. She breathes in their sweet smell. She digs her fingers in the soil like roots.

"When I grow up, I want to be a plant," Pamela tells the flowers.

Pamela talks to plants all the time. Her parents don't pay much attention to her. She doesn't have any school friends. Only the plants are her friends.

As Pamela gets older, she reads everything she can about trees, flowers and other plants. There are so many types!

She learns that there are people who study plants. They are called botanists.

"I am going to be a botanist!" Pamela says.

Pamela studies hard. Finally, she goes to university to follow her dream.

One of her teachers is a man called Dr Jason Woodrue. He knows a lot about plants. Pamela is happy when he takes a special interest in her.

At last, she thinks. *I can talk to someone who loves plants as much as I do!*

But Dr Woodrue has a secret.
He's doing dangerous experiments.
He tricks Pamela into one. In a
hidden lab, he injects her with
plant poisons. He wants to make
her half-plant, half-human.

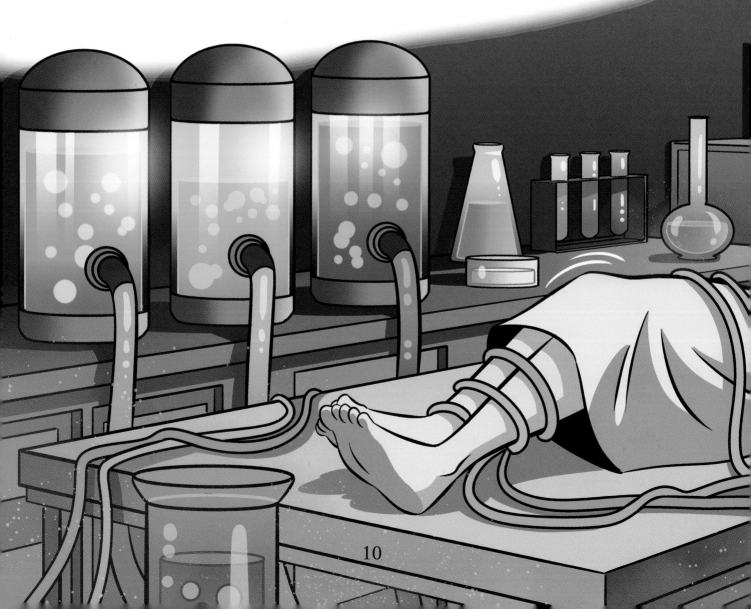

The experiment goes wrong.
Pamela becomes very ill. She stays
in hospital for six months.

Pamela finally recovers. But she is not the same. Dr Woodrue's plant poisons blossom inside her. They give her some very unusual powers.

One day, Pamela sees a wilted flower. She touches its leaves. She wishes it would grow and be strong.

WHOOOSH!

Suddenly the flower opens. The leaves pop up. The plant grows huge!

I did that with just my mind,

Pamela realizes.

Pamela tries to discover what else she can do.

She finds she can mutate plants. She can mix them to create new types. She can make fantastic shapes.

No poison harms Pamela. In fact, her body now creates them! She can poison a person with just a kiss.

Her body also makes powerful pheromones. These chemicals let her control people's minds.

Most amazing of all, Pamela can *hear* plants! She hears them all over the planet.

Rainforest trees cry out as bulldozers plough them down. A struggling seedling moans as a skyscraper blocks the sun.

My friends! They're in so much pain! Pamela thinks. *Humans are hurting them!*

The plants' pain makes her angry.

Pamela decides to do something about it.

"I'll make humans pay," Pamela says. "I'll steal their money and use it to protect plants."

She creates a special look and a new name.

"I am . . . Poison Ivy!" she declares.

Poison Ivy begins her life of crime in Gotham City. She keeps her promise to rob the rich to save the plants. She crashes a party full of wealthy people.

Ivy spreads spores on the crowd. **POP! POP! POP!** The spores grow into poison mushrooms.

"Give me your cash and jewels if you want the cure!" Poison Ivy says.

The party guests pay up. But that's not enough for the Super-Villain.

"Pay me one million dollars, or I'll release a more powerful spore on all of Gotham," Poison Ivy says.

But as she leaves the party, a dark shadow follows her.

It's Batman!

SMAAAASH!

Batman bursts into Poison Ivy's
secret hideout.

"I can't let you carry out your threat," Batman tells the villain.

"My plants will make mulch out of you!" Poison Ivy replies.

She attacks with giant vines.

WHOOOSH! WHOOOSH!

The vines wrap around the hero.

They pull him close to Poison Ivy.

"How about a little poison kiss?" Ivy asks.

"No thanks," Batman says.

SNIIIK! SNIIIK!

Batman cuts the vines around him with a sharp Batarang. Then he quickly uses a Batrope to tie up Poison Ivy.

FWIIIP! She can't move.

"I give up," Ivy says. "For now."

Batman takes Poison Ivy to Arkham Asylum. It is a special prison for Super-Villains.

"I won't stay in this cell for long," Ivy says. "Plants always find their way back into the sunshine."

Poison Ivy escapes from Arkham many times. She continues her mission to steal from the rich and give to the plants.

Batman is always there to stop Poison Ivy. He is fearless when facing her mutant plants.

Ivy respects Batman as a foe. The villain sometimes even flirts with the hero.

"Don't you think I'm as beautiful as a rose, Batman?" Ivy asks.

She tries to use her mind control on him to get away. But Batman is always on guard against the danger.

At first, Poison Ivy's life of crime is lonely. She is on her own, just like when she was a kid.

Then Ivy meets Harley Quinn. The clownish crook is sad. Her boyfriend, the Joker, has broken up with her.

Ivy wants to cheer up Harley.
"Let's have some fun. Let's go on a
crime spree!" she says.

They burst in on a meeting of rich
businessmen. Harley drops some seed
pods. Then Ivy uses her powers.

WHOOOSH! WHOOOSH!

Vines shoot out from the pods.
The plants wrap up the men while
Ivy and Harley loot everything.

The pair go on to steal rare plants. They rob jewellery shops. Their success makes Harley feel better. She smiles when the newspapers call them the New Queens of Crime!

Ivy and Harley team up many times afterwards. The crazy criminal makes Ivy laugh, and Harley likes Ivy too. At last, Poison Ivy has a real friend.

There are times when Poison Ivy
teams up with other Super-Villains.

She works with mighty criminals
such as Gorilla Grodd and Bizarro.
But only if it helps to achieve
her own goals.

When there is a major threat to plants, Poison Ivy will even join forces with Super Heroes.

She fights with Black Canary and Batgirl to save a rare forest from wrecking robots. Still, Ivy always has her own interests in mind.

It doesn't matter if Poison Ivy is using her amazing powers to battle Batman or to save the environment.

One thing never changes for the Queen of Green.

Poison Ivy loves her plants and is always true to her roots.

Poison Ivy

REAL NAME: DR PAMELA ISLEY

CRIMINAL NAME: POISON IVY

ROLE: SUPER-VILLAIN

BASE: GOTHAM CITY

Poison Ivy is no garden-variety crook. A failed experiment with plant poisons gave her incredible abilities. Plants grow and mutate at her command. No poison can harm her, but her touch is toxic to humans. She loves plants more than people and calls herself the Queen of Green.

THE AUTHOR

LAURIE S. SUTTON has been reading comics since she was a kid. She grew up to become an editor for Marvel, DC Comics, Starblaze and Tekno Comics. She has written Adam Strange for DC, Star Trek: Voyager for Marvel, plus Star Trek: Deep Space Nine and Witch Hunter for Malibu Comics. There are long boxes of comics in her wardrobe where there should be clothing and shoes. Laurie has lived all over the world and currently lives in Florida, USA.

THE ILLUSTRATOR

DARIO BRIZUELA works traditionally and digitally in many different illustration styles. His work can be found in a wide range of properties, including Star Wars Tales, DC Super Hero Girls, DC Super Friends, Transformers, Scooby-Doo! Team-Up and more. Brizuela lives in Buenos Aires, Argentina.

GLOSSARY

botanist person who studies plant life

experiment scientific test to try out an idea

mission important work that you feel strongly you are meant to do

mutate go through or cause a change in a living thing's genetic make-up, giving it new characteristics

pheromone chemical produced by animals that is often used to send messages and attract others

poison substance that can harm living things

protect keep safe

spore something made by fungi that is like a seed and can grow new fungi

spree period of time when you do a lot of something

DISCUSSION QUESTIONS

Write down your answers. Look back at the story for help.

QUESTION 1.

Imagine Pamela Isley hadn't met Dr Woodrue. How would her life be different? How would it be the same?

QUESTION 2.

Why do you think Poison Ivy chose that as her Super-Villain name? Support your answer with examples from the story.

QUESTION 3.

Poison Ivy wants to protect plants. What do you think of this goal? What are other ways she could use her powers to help the environment?

QUESTION 4.

What is your favourite illustration in this book? Explain your choice.

READ THEM ALL!!

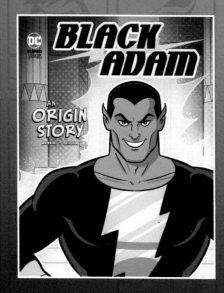